THE HATING BOOK

by CHARLOTTE ZOLOTOW

Pictures by Ben Shecter

■ HarperTrophy®
A Division of HarperCollinsPublishers

Library of Congress Catalog Card Number: 69-14444
ISBN 0-06-026923-5
ISBN 0-06-026924-3 (lib. bdg.)
ISBN 0-06-443197-5 (pbk.)

To Nina

I hate hate hated
my friend.

When I moved over in the school bus,
she sat somewhere else.

When her point broke in arithmetic
and I passed her my pencil,
she took Peter's instead.

"Ask her," my mother said,
"ask your friend why."

8

But I wouldn't,
I couldn't,
I'd rather die.

9

What if she should say
Oh, please, just go away.
You're ugly and dumb.
Being with you
was never fun.

Oh, I hated my friend.

When it was her turn to wash the board,
she didn't ask me to help.

When it was time to choose teams,
she didn't choose me.
And when I made a basket
and everyone else yelled *YA A A A*,
she turned away.

Oh, I hated my friend.

When I went to walk home with her,
she had already gone.

When she took her dog out
and I whistled to him,
she put him on a leash
and led him away.

Oh, I hated my friend.

"Ask her," my mother said,
"ask her why."

22

I couldn't,
I'd rather die.
No—
if that's the way she's going to be,
it's quite okay with me.

"Ask her," my mother said,
"ask and see..."

24

I wouldn't,
I couldn't.
But
maybe...

"You've been so rotten," I said.
"Why?"
  She looked as though she'd cry.
"It's you," she said. "Last week
  when I wore my new dress,
  Sue said Jane said you said
  I looked like a freak."
"I did not!
  I said you looked *neat*!"

She looked straight at me for a while,
and then we both began to smile.
My friend said, "Hey,
maybe tomorrow we can play?"
"Oh, yes," I said, "OKAY!"

I didn't hate her anyway.
I wish it were tomorrow.

32